PUFFIN B

Not Quit

MERMA PARTY

Linda Chapman lives in Leicestershire with her family and two Bernese mountain dogs. When she is not writing she spends her time looking after her two young daughters, horse riding and teaching drama.

Not Quite a Mermaid

MERMAID PARTY

LINDA CHAPMAN

Illustrated by Dawn Apperley

PUFFIN

PUFFIN BOOKS

Published by the Penguin Group
Penguin Books Ltd, 80 Strand, London WC2R 0RL, England
Penguin Group (USA) Inc., 375 Hudson Street, New York,
New York 10014, USA
Penguin Group (Canada), 90 Eglinton Avenue East, Suite 700, Toronto, Ontario,
Canada M4P 2Y3 (a division of Pearson Penguin Canada Inc.)
Penguin Ireland, 25 St Stephen's Green, Dublin 2, Ireland
(a division of Penguin Books Ltd)
Penguin Group (Australia), 250 Camberwell Road, Camberwell,
Victoria 3124, Australia (a division of Pearson Australia Group Pty Ltd)
Penguin Books India Pvt Ltd, 11 Community Centre, Panchsheel Park,
New Delhi – 110 017, India
Penguin Group (NZ), cnr Airborne and Rosedale Roads, Albany,
Auckland 1310, New Zealand (a division of Pearson New Zealand Ltd)
Penguin Books (South Africa) (Pty) Ltd, 24 Sturdee Avenue,
Rosebank, Johannesburg 2196, South Africa

Penguin Books Ltd, Registered Offices: 80 Strand, London WC2R 0RL, England

www.penguin.com

First published 2006
1

Text copyright © Linda Chapman, 2006
Illustrations copyright © Dawn Apperley, 2006
All rights reserved

The moral right of the author and illustrator has been asserted

Set in Palatino
Made and printed in England by Clays Ltd, St Ives plc

British Library Cataloguing in Publication Data
A CIP catalogue record for this book is available from the British Library

ISBN-13: 978–0–14132–052–6
ISBN-10: 0–141–32052–4

To seven friends who love mermaids –
Amy, Anna, Charlotte, Georgia,
Iola, Jessica and Lucy

Contents

Chapter One

'I can't do this!' Electra the mermaid exclaimed. She tried again to poke the end of the seaweed through a pretty white whelk shell but the seaweed just flopped uselessly to one side. 'Stupid seaweed!' Electra threw it down and pushed back her long red hair in frustration.

Sam and Sasha, the mer-twins, and Nerissa, one of Electra's other school friends, were threading shells too. They looked up in surprise.

'What's the matter?' Sam asked.

'The seaweed won't go through the shell!' Electra grumbled crossly.

'It's easy,' Sasha said. 'Look.' She took the shell from Electra and, after a few seconds careful poking and prodding, managed to thread it on to the seaweed. 'You just have to be patient and take your time.'

Electra sighed. She wasn't very good at being patient and taking her time. She liked diving and swimming and having adventures.

Just then a grey head popped up out of the water. It was Splash,

Electra's pet dolphin. 'Hi, Splash,' Electra grinned.

Splash swam over to the rocks Electra was sitting on and nudged her curiously. 'What are you doing, Electra?'

'Making decorations.' Electra looked ruefully at the long strings of shells that the others had threaded and then at her own piece of seaweed with just three shells on it. 'But I'm not very good at it.'

'Come diving with me then,' Splash said.

'I can't,' replied Electra. 'The grown-ups have asked us to make these decorations for the New Year's Day ceremony this afternoon.'

Every New Year's Day, the merpeople who lived on the coral reef in the waters around Mermaid Island had a grand ceremony to say thank you to the sea for all the things it had brought to them throughout the year. The ceremony was held in an enormous underwater grotto in the deepest part of the reef. Afterwards there was always a big party with music, dancing and a delicious feast.

'I can't wait till the party,' Sam said. 'It's brilliant we're old enough to go this year, isn't it?'

Electra nodded. Merchildren were only allowed to stay for the party

when they reached Year Four at school and this was the first year Electra and the others had been old enough. She was really looking forward to it.

'I wonder if one of us will be chosen to be Queen at the ceremony?' Nerissa

said. One of the youngest mermaids was always chosen to be Queen of the New Year. The Queen wore a glittering pink crystal crown and a long cloak embroidered with mother-of-pearl sequins.

Sasha dreamily twirled the single plait in her wavy blonde hair. 'I'd really love to be Queen.'

'Me too,' Electra sighed.

'Yuck – soppy!' Sam pulled a face.

Electra grinned at him. 'Oh, Sam!' she teased. 'I think you'd look lovely in a pink crown!'

Sam chucked a handful of seaweed at her. Electra squealed as it flopped on her head. Grabbing more seaweed, she threw it back, giggling.

'Stop it, you two!' Nerissa exclaimed crossly. 'We need to get on with these decorations. My mum said that the mermaid who's the most helpful on New Year's Day is the one who gets chosen to be Queen.'

Electra stopped throwing seaweed and stared at Nerissa. 'Really?'

'I'm going to do loads of shells then,' Sasha said hastily. 'Come on, Electra. You'd better hurry up.'

But Electra didn't do anything. Nerissa's words had sent an idea spinning into her mind.

'Oh no,' Sam said, catching sight of the grin that was suddenly pulling at the corners of her mouth. 'I know that look. You've had one of your ideas again, haven't you, Electra?'

'Yes!' Electra's blue eyes shone. 'If it's the mermaid who's the most helpful who gets to be Queen then why don't we stop doing these boring decorations and go to the underwater grotto?'

The others stared at her.

'Why would we do that?' Nerissa asked.

'There's bound to be loads that needs doing down there,' Electra replied. 'We'll be able to be much more help than if we stay here.'

'But we were told to make decorations,' Sasha said uncertainly.

'There are lots of other people making decorations.' Electra waved across the rocks to where the rest of their class sat threading shells on to seaweed. 'I bet we'll be much more help in the grotto. The grown-ups will be really pleased to see us,' she went on, looking persuasively at Sasha and Nerissa. 'In fact, maybe we'll be so helpful down there they'll decide to make us *all* Queen!' She looked at Sam. 'And it'll be much more fun than threading shells on boring seaweed.'

Nerissa, Sam and Sasha hesitated.

'Come on,' Electra urged them.

'No. I'm going to stay here,' Nerissa decided. 'The grotto's really deep down in the reef. We shouldn't swim that far on our own without our parents.'

Sasha shivered. 'I'm staying here too.'

Electra looked at Sasha's twin. 'What about you, Sam?'

Sam looked almost tempted but then he shook his head. 'No. You know how much trouble we got into last time we went off by ourselves – we almost got eaten by sharks.'

Electra remembered that day only too well. She and the twins had swum outside of the reef, on an adventure, into the deep sea but two sharks had chased them and they had only just escaped. She quickly pushed the memory away. This would be different. The grotto was deep down in the water but it was the reef. No sharks would be a get them there.

'It'll be fine,' she said. But they didn't look convinced. 'You'll come with me, won't you, Splash?' Electra asked.

Splash's dark eyes sparkled. 'Of course. It sounds like fun to me.' He dived into the water. 'Come on!'

'See you later!' Electra called to the others. 'I'm off to be helpful *and* to be chosen to be Queen.' And standing up, she plunged off the rocks and swam after Splash.

Chapter Two

Electra kicked hard with her feet. 'Wait, Splash!' she called, wishing for about the millionth time in her life that she had a tail like all her friends. It would make swimming so much easier!

'Sorry, I forgot,' Splash said.

'That's OK,' Electra said as she reached him. Being so adventurous wasn't the only thing that made Electra different from her friends. She also had feet and legs instead of a tail! This was because she had been born a human. The merpeople had found her, when she was a tiny baby, floating in a boat, eight years ago after a dreadful storm. They had given her sea powder so she could breathe underwater and then had brought her up as one of them. Maris, a young adult mermaid, had adopted her. *My gift from the sea*, Maris often whispered, when she kissed Electra goodnight.

Electra smiled as she thought about it. She couldn't imagine having a different mum now, though sometimes she had a feeling Maris *could* imagine having a different daughter. Particularly when Electra got into trouble – which seemed to be most of the time.

'Why can't you be content to sit on the rocks and play tick in the shallow

waters like the other mermaids?'
Maris had sighed only the night before
as Electra had confessed that a giant
clam had eaten her homework book
when she'd been exploring the reef
after school. She'd shaken her head.

'You really have to stop getting into scrapes, Electra.'

The words echoed through Electra's mind now. What would her mum think of her latest plan of swimming down to the grotto? Electra pushed the thought aside. She was going to be helpful. Of course her mum wouldn't mind.

'The grotto's at the deepest part of the reef, isn't it?' Splash said, as the turquoise waters darkened to a deeper indigo blue around them. It never got really dark in the waters around Mermaid Island because the sea wasn't deep enough.

'Yes,' Electra replied, as they swam around the coral. 'We need to go right down to the seabed.'

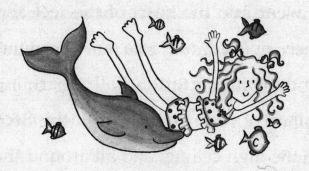

They swam on, weaving through shoals of stripy fish and past herds of tiny, bobbing sea horses until they reached the place where the reef was the thickest. A cave had formed in the coral wall. Electra swam into it. At the back of it, instead of a solid wall there was a wide tunnel.

She and Splash swam into the tunnel. It twisted round a corner as it went into the heart of the reef and then opened out into an enormous underwater grotto. Tall sparkling pillars of rock reached from the floor to the high ceiling, and all around the walls were tunnels leading away in different directions. Four huge bowls of mermaid fire had been placed around the grotto. Mermaid fire was a special magic fire that the mermaids collected from the seabed. They used it for cooking and for lighting up dark places. The grotto walls glittered and shone in the light of the green flames.

'Wow! This is amazing!' Splash

whistled. He hadn't lived in the waters of Mermaid Island for long and he'd never been in the grotto before.

'I wonder where everyone is,' Electra said. 'I thought all the adults would be here.'

The adults had obviously been in the grotto because a huge table had been set up along one wall and there were boxes of decorations piled on the floor.

'There's a note on the table,' Splash pointed out.

Electra swam over to it. *'Gone to get the musical instruments. Back soon to put decorations up,'* she read.

'Never mind,' Splash whistled. 'I guess we just wait till someone comes back.'

'Unless,' said Electra thoughtfully, 'we put the decorations up by ourselves. Imagine how pleased the adults would be!'

'Yes,' Splash said. 'So pleased that you might get to be Queen.' Swimming over to the crates, he nudged one of the boxes with his nose.

Electra looked at the boxes. There were rolls and rolls of green, purple and pink seaweed streamers. 'We need to hang them around the roof on the bits of rock that are sticking out,' she said, looking up at the ceiling.

'Why don't you sit on my back?' suggested Splash. 'You'll be able to carry loads in one go and it'll mean we won't have to keep swimming down here every time to get more.'

'Good idea,' Electra agreed. She picked up an armful of pink and purple seaweed ribbons and climbed on to Splash's back. He swam up to the roof and she hooked the end of one piece of seaweed on to a peg of rock. The loose end hung down towards the cave floor. It waved gently in the water.

'It looks good,' Electra said, pleased. 'Next one!'

Splash swooped around the cave, stopping every now and then so Electra could fasten the end of a streamer to another rocky peg.

'This is great!' gasped Electra as she and Splash charged around.

'Whee!' said Splash, diving down through the water and twisting through the seaweed streamers. 'I'm having fun!'

Back and forward they went until at last they hung the last streamer in place. 'Wow!' Electra said, looking round at the mass of streamers hanging down from the roof. 'It looks amazing!'

'Um, yes.' Splash hesitated. 'Electra, you don't think that there are maybe . . . well, too *many* streamers?'

Electra bit her lip. There *were* a lot

of streamers. In fact, so many that in places you could hardly see the grotto. 'I guess it doesn't usually look like this when we have the ceremony,' she said, peering through the curtain of seaweed, but then she brightened up. 'But I'm sure everyone will be pleased!'

Just then there was the sound of voices in one of the tunnels leading into the grotto.

'It's the adults!' Electra exclaimed. 'They've come back!'

'These boxes of instruments are heavy,' said a voice that Electra recognized as belonging to Solon, her schoolteacher.

'Nearly there,' said a woman's voice.

Mum, thought Electra.

'We'll need to get the decorations up as quickly as possible,' she heard

Ronan, the twins' dad, say. 'We don't want the ceremony to start late. I'll start on the streamers and then . . .' He swam into the grotto straight into a tangle of streamers and broke off with a shocked gasp.

'Oh!' Electra's mum exclaimed as she swam out of the tunnel and got tangled up too. In her surprise she

dropped the box she was carrying. There was a bang and then more crashes as the other adults swam into the grotto, got caught in the streamers and lost their grip on the boxes they were holding. The air filled with shouts and cries and crashes.

'What's happened?' Solon shouted. 'Who put all these streamers up?'

'My flute's broken.'

'And my drum.'

Electra gulped. The adults didn't look pleased. 'Uh-oh,' she whispered to Splash.

Just then, Maris spotted her. 'Electra!' she exclaimed. 'What are *you* doing here?'

Chapter Three

Maris stared at Electra and then round at the chaos in the grotto. The other merpeople were picking themselves off the floor and examining the musical instruments they had dropped.

'Um . . .' Electra began.

'Oh, Electra,' Maris said slowly. 'Please don't tell me you and Splash had something to do with this.'

'We were just trying to help,' Electra said.

'*Help!*' Maris cried. 'Look at the mess! We can't have the ceremony when we can't even see the grotto. Now we're going to have to take down all the decorations and start again, not to mention mending the musical instruments.'

'We haven't got time to take them all down,' Solon said crossly. 'We'll just have to sort out the ones in the middle of the grotto where the ceremony takes place. The ones at the edge will have to stay as they are.'

'Electra!' Maris said. 'You've been a real nuisance. Go home!'

Electra saw her dreams of becoming the Queen disappearing. 'Can't I help to clear up?' she begged. 'I didn't mean to make more work for you.'

'Electra *was* just trying to help,' Ronan put in. Electra looked at him hopefully. 'Why don't you let her stay, Maris? There's lots to do.'

Maris hesitated.

'Please, Mum,' Electra begged. 'I'll be as good as gold.'

Maris nodded. 'All right. You and Splash can stay. You can sweep the floors of the caves. But no more getting into trouble. OK?'

'OK!' Electra agreed, her heart leaping. Maybe she could still prove herself to be the most helpful mermaid after all. 'We'll sweep the floors really, really well. I promise. Come on, Splash!'

She and Splash swam towards the caves. Picking up a handful of seaweed, Electra began to smooth out the sandy floor.

Splash brushed for a while with his tail but then he got bored and began to nose around at the back of the cave. 'Where do you think these caves go?' he said. 'This one turns into a sort of tunnel.'

'Well, the tunnels on the other side of the grotto lead back towards

Mermaid Island,' Electra said. 'So I guess these here must lead out towards the deep sea.'

'That sounds exciting,' Splash said.

Their eyes met.

'Do you think we should go and check them out?' Electra said with a grin. 'I mean, there might be something dangerous in the tunnels. We *should* make sure they're safe. That would be a very helpful thing to do.'

'You're right,' Splash agreed with a flick of his tail. 'Come on!'

They headed down the tunnel. It was almost pitch black and Electra had to magic a ball of mermaid fire from the floor of the tunnel so they could see. Touching her hands to the rocky bottom, she whispered, *'From the deep of the sea, mermaid fire come to me.'*

Crackling green fire flowed out of the rock into her cupped hands. It formed into a glowing ball, lighting up the gloom.

A viperfish came swimming towards them. Its black scales shone eerily and its mouth opened to show a display of sharp needle-like teeth. Electra tucked her feet up high; she didn't want it to mistake her toes for a fish! They swam on. There were all sorts of strange creatures in the dark tunnel – a flat stripy eel that looked like a piece of ribbon, a rat-tailed fish with a long, thin tail and a giant tube worm wriggling along the floor. Finally they reached the end of the

tunnel. There was an old wall, built out of coral, blocking the way.

'I think the deep sea is just on the other side of the wall,' Splash said, nosing around it.

'I bet the wall's been put here to keep out anything very dangerous from the deep sea,' Electra said. 'Let's check the other tunnels and see if they've got walls too.'

They swam back and went into another tunnel. It also had a wall at the end, but the tunnel they explored next had a wall that had crumbled away leaving an enormous gaping hole.

'The deep sea!' Splash said, swimming through the hole. Electra followed him.

It was strange to be on the other side of the coral wall. The sea stretched above and below her. What might be lurking nearby? A picture of a shark flashed into her mind again. There could be whole families of them swimming around.

She shivered suddenly. She liked adventures but not when they involved sharks! 'Come on, we should probably go back,' she said.

Splash nodded. 'We should tell the

adults about this hole. It needs to be blocked up.'

They swam back along the tunnel.

As they neared the grotto, a side tunnel that ran off from the main one caught Electra's eye. There was something in it – a dark shadowy mound about as long as two adult mermen. It was blocking most of the tunnel. She paused and peered closer. Was it a rock?

It was a very strange purply colour and it didn't look hard like rock but sort of soft and squishy.

Electra swam closer.

'What are you doing?' Splash called.

'There's something down here,' hissed Electra. 'Come and see.'

Splash swam over.

'What do you think it is?' Electra whispered.

'I don't know,' Splash replied.

'It's sort of octopus-shaped,' Electra said, looking at the torpedo-shaped mound. 'Maybe it's a giant squid.'

'It can't be a squid. It doesn't have any tentacles,' Splash pointed out.

Electra glanced at him. 'Do you dare me to go closer?'

Splash nodded. 'Go on.'

Electra swam cautiously towards the mound. Was it alive or dead? Was it a creature or a rock? She reached out to touch it. Suddenly a single giant black eye blinked open in front of her.

Electra yelled in shock.

For a split second the creature stared back at her with a look of horror and then a blinding flash of brilliant blue-green light lit up the water with the power of a lightning bolt.

Electra ducked. In a cloud of bubbles, the giant creature burst into the grotto. Electra heard startled yells and shouts and raced to the cave entrance. A cloud of black ink was shooting out of the creature. It went every-where – over the decorations, the table, the people . . .

'Oh no!' Electra gasped.

The creature swerved across the grotto, knocking over four merpeople and sending a pile of boxes crashing to the floor.

Electra and Splash dived out of the way just in time as it swooshed past them into the tunnel. It disappeared towards the deep sea.

'Electra!' Maris shouted. 'Come out of there right now!'

Electra looked at Splash in alarm. 'Whoops,' she gulped. 'Looks like we're really in trouble now!'

Chapter Four

Electra and Splash swam slowly out of the cave.

'What's going on?' Maris exclaimed.

'I don't know,' Electra said. 'I saw that thing and had a look at it and it just sort of exploded with fright.' She looked back down the tunnel. 'What *was* it?'

'A Dana squid,' Merrick, the chief of the merpeople, replied. His blond hair and beard and silvery tail were streaked black with ink. 'They're a type of giant squid.'

'But it didn't have any tentacles,' frowned Electra.

'Dana squid only have very short

tentacles,' Merrick told her. 'They are very shy, gentle creatures and we hardly ever see them. When they're frightened their arm-tips flash with light and they shoot out a cloud of black ink to startle away any attackers. I guess that's what happened. It thought you were attacking it.'

'I was just trying to see what it was,' said Electra.

'The decorations are ruined,' one of the other mermaids complained.

'We're going to have to start getting everything ready all over again,' Solon put in, looking at Electra crossly.

'Come on, everyone. Let's get a move on or we'll never be ready in time.'

The adults started to swim away and clear up. Electra let out a sigh of relief. But then she saw her mum's face and her heart sank. Maris looked very angry.

'Electra! I thought I told you not to get into any more trouble!'

'I was just trying to . . .'

'Don't even think about saying you were trying to help!' her mum exclaimed. 'You were supposed to be sweeping the floors, not disturbing giant squid! I've a good mind to send you home so you miss the party.'

Electra looked at her in horror. 'Please don't. I'll be good. I promise.'

Maris pushed a hand through her hair. 'All right, but as a punishment you can clear the sea urchins from the

grotto. Put them right at the back of the caves so no one sits on them and stay out of everyone's way!'

Electra sighed. Clearing sea urchins away was no fun at all – they were prickly and their spines usually jabbed into your fingers when you tried to pick them up – but at least she wasn't being sent home.

'Guess I'm not going to be Queen now,' she muttered to Splash as she started searching the rocks for sea urchins. Seeing one, she picked it up. Its prickles jabbed into her hand. 'Ow!' she exclaimed. Suddenly she remembered something. 'The wall!

I haven't told anyone about the hole in the wall. I'd better tell Mum.'

Dropping the sea urchin, she swam quickly back to Maris. 'Mum! There's something I've got to –'

'Electra,' Maris said firmly. 'I told

you to stay out of the way.'

'But, Mum . . .' Electra protested.

'Do you want me to send you home?' Maris demanded.

'No, but –'

'Then start clearing those sea urchins and don't stop until the ceremony starts. You're being punished, remember?'

Electra swam back to Splash. 'She wouldn't listen!'

'Try Ronan,' Splash suggested.

Electra swam over to the twins' dad. 'Ronan . . .'

'Not now, Electra,' Ronan said as he carried a heavy blue basket sponge to the middle of the grotto. It was filled with magic sea powder for the thanking-the-sea ceremony.

'But –'

'Electra, I'm busy. I don't want to spill this.'

Seeing her mum glance over in her direction, Electra quickly swam away.

'What shall we do?' she said to Splash.

'Don't worry about it,' Splash

advised. 'The wall must have been crumbling for years and nothing's happened yet. Sharks won't come through it unless they're following something. You can tell everyone about the wall tomorrow and they can mend it then.'

'I guess,' Electra agreed. With a sigh she began to look for sea urchins again.

Gradually the grotto was made ready for the ceremony. The decorations were cleaned up with some mermaid magic, the musical instruments were set out and plates of food were placed on the table. There was a cake right in the middle – it had five tiers of white icing and it was decorated with pink and lilac sugar shells and tiny starfish. Electra felt her tummy rumble. It looked delicious!

More and more people started to arrive. Electra saw Sam, Sasha and Nerissa swim into the grotto with Nerissa's mum and dad. She waved but didn't dare go over in case her mum saw her.

'I hate sea urchins,' she muttered to Splash, ducking through some streamers as she carried two spiky urchins towards one of the tunnels.

'Don't go in that tunnel,' Splash said suddenly. 'Look!'

Electra stopped. The Dana squid had come back from the deep sea. It was settling down in a crevasse in the tunnel entrance.

'Maybe I'll put these into a different cave,' Electra said hastily.

They found another cave on the other side of the grotto and she put the sea urchins there instead. Electra tucked them right to the back of the cave so that no one would be in danger of sitting on one.

Just then there was the sound of a conch shell being blown in the grotto. 'The ceremony's about to start,' Electra said, glancing round and seeing the other merpeople starting to gather together in a circle in the middle of the grotto. 'Let's go and join in.'

They went to the cave entrance. As

they swam out into the grotto, Splash stopped dead and gave a whistle of alarm.

'What is it?' Electra said. She followed his gaze and gasped.

On the other side of the grotto, four sinister dark-grey shapes were swimming out of the tunnel with the broken wall. Their beady black eyes were fixed hungrily on the circle of merpeople in front of them.

'Oh no,' Electra whispered in horror. 'Sharks!'

Chapter Five

The sharks began to swim silently towards the group of merpeople. They opened their mouths showing row upon row of sharp yellow teeth. It looked like they were laughing.

'Mum!' Electra screamed as the

sharks snaked towards the merpeople.

'Ronan! Merrick! Sharks!'

The merpeople swung round and screamed as they saw the sharks. Splitting up, the four sharks began to

circle quickly round the group. They darted at the merpeople, snapping their jaws.

'No!' Electra gasped as she saw a shark just miss Sasha's arm.

'We've got to do something!' Splash whistled.

'I know. But what?' Electra cried. Guilt crashed down on her. 'They must have got in through that hole in

the wall. It's all my fault. I should have told someone about it!'

Screams and cries filled the air as the merpeople huddled together. Electra could see Sam, Sasha, Ronan and her mum hanging on to each other.

One of the sharks lunged at Maris. Maris screamed and shrank back,

shielding the twins with her tail. The shark lunged again.

Electra felt sick with fear. What was she going to do?

Beside her she could feel Splash trembling. Sharks had killed his mother only a few months ago. 'They must have followed the Dana squid here,' he said, watching in horror as the sharks began to close in on the merpeople.

An idea suddenly flashed into Electra's head. 'That's it!' she said. Grabbing his fin, she climbed on his back. 'The Dana squid! Come on, Splash!'

'What are we going to do?' Splash gasped.

'Go to the cave where the squid is!' replied Electra.

'But if we go in it will frighten the squid and then it'll –'

'Trust me, Splash,' Electra said, gripping his sides with her knees. 'Please! Just do it!'

Splash didn't need telling twice. He set off across the grotto like an arrow.

'Electra! What are you doing?' Electra heard her mum cry as they swerved around the sharks towards the cave. 'Swim away with Splash! Escape while you can.'

But Electra knew there was no way she could leave her family and friends in such danger.

Splash dived into the cave. The Dana squid was lying quietly in the crevasse. 'Wake up!' Electra yelled at it. 'Please, wake up!'

The squid's eye blinked open. At the sight of Electra and Splash heading straight towards it, it jumped in fright. Bubbles shot from behind it and it darted into the grotto. As it did so, its two arm-tips exploded with light. Brilliant blue-green light flashed through the water. The sharks swung round in surprise. As the squid saw them, its eye widened.

'Duck!' Electra yelled to the other merpeople as the alarmed squid blasted a jet of black ink straight at the sharks and then raced across the grotto and into another tunnel.

The sharks scattered in confusion, shaking their heads in the black ink.

'Go on! Go away you horrible things!' Electra shouted. Her eyes fell on the musical instruments table. 'Go to the music table, Splash!' He raced over and she grabbed the cymbals. 'Now head for the sharks.'

As Splash darted through the water, Electra banged the cymbals loudly and shouted for all she was worth.

The sharks stared at her in alarm.

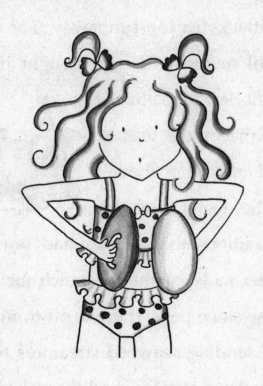

They weren't used to seeing mermaids riding on dolphins. Particularly not mermaids with legs. They hesitated as if unsure whether to attack her or run away. For one awful moment Electra thought they might decide to attack but just then there was a loud *crack* from above!

The weight of the decorations that Electra had put up earlier had become too much for one of the stone pegs. It broke off from the roof sending seaweed streamers tumbling down over the sharks' grey bodies.

The sharks panicked. Fighting free of the seaweed that was wrapping around their fins and jaws, they gave up on having mermaids for supper and charged away down the tunnel as fast as they could go.

For a moment there was silence and then everyone started to talk at once. Children cried, people shouted.

'They've gone! The sharks have gone!'

'Hurray!'

'Oh, Electra!' Maris cried. 'I'm so glad you're OK.'

Electra dived off Splash and swam

over to meet her mum. 'I'm glad you're safe too,' she said, feeling shaky with shock.

'You saved the day!' Maris said, hugging her so tightly that Electra could hardly breathe.

'Thank you, Electra!' Merrick, the chief, said, swimming over with the other mer-people. 'You were very brave.'

'You were wonderful!' Solon said, patting her on the back.

'You saved us,' Sasha said, her face pale.

Electra shivered. 'It was horrible. I thought you were all going to be eaten. There's a hole in one of the

tunnel walls. The sharks must have come in that way. I tried to tell you about it,' she said, looking at her mum and Ronan. 'But you wouldn't listen.'

'Oh, Electra,' Maris said. 'I'm so sorry.'

'I'll repair the hole right away,' Ronan told her.

'It won't take very long,' Merrick put in. 'Not if we use some mermaid magic.' He took a handful of sea powder from the basket sponge and passed it to Ronan.

'I'll have it fixed in ten minutes,' said Ronan, swimming off.

'That just gives us time to get ready for the ceremony again, and –' Merrick looked at Electra – 'to choose the Queen of the New Year.'

Electra gasped. 'Who . . . who's it going to be?' She held her breath, hardly able to bear waiting for the answer.

Merrick's face was solemn. 'Well, after everything that has happened today, I think it has to be . . .'

Electra's heart sunk as she thought of the chaos she and Splash had caused earlier on.

'. . . you!' Merrick finished with a smile.

All around them, the merpeople cheered and clapped.

'And now,' Merrick said, holding up his hand to quieten the noise, 'it's time to get ready for the ceremony!'

Chapter Six

Ten minutes later the ceremony began. 'Fellow merpeople, I welcome you to our New Year's Day celebrations,' Merrick announced as the last notes of Solon's conch shell echoed away. 'We shall start as always by giving our thanks to the sea.'

Standing at Merrick's side, wearing a pink crown and a robe that glittered with mother-of-pearl sequins, Electra could hardly contain her excitement.

'I will ask our Queen of the New Year to start the ceremony,' Merrick said. He put his hand on Electra's arm. 'Think carefully what you would like to thank the sea for.'

Electra took a deep breath. Walking to the basket sponge, she took a few grains of sea powder. 'I thank the sea for the food it gives us,' she said in a clear voice. Splash whistled at her. She grinned at him. 'And for all the adventures it brings us too,' she added with a grin. She let the powder go. It floated away, turning from blue to purple to pink and finally

dissolving into the sea.

She stepped back beside Merrick.

Maris went next. 'I thank the sea for the gift it gave to me eight years ago,' she said softly, her eyes on Electra. 'A very special daughter.'

Electra swallowed.

Letting her sea powder go, Maris walked over and put an arm round her shoulders. 'Whatever I say, I never want you to change,' she said, hugging Electra. 'I love you.'

'Love you too, Mum,' Electra whispered, hugging her back.

Suddenly Splash popped up between them. 'What about me?'

Electra and Maris grinned. 'We love you as well, Splash,' they both chorused, stroking his head.

Standing together they watched as one by one the other merpeople stepped forward and said their own thanks. When the last person finished they stood in a circle and Solon blew a deep note on his horn to end the ceremony.

'And now it is time for the feast,' Merrick declared.

Electra sat on the throne at the head of the table for the feast, trying not to stare too much at the enormous cake on the table! Everywhere looked so beautiful. See-through jellyfish and tiny firefly squid about half the size of her hand danced through the water, their bodies lit up like bright candles. The streamers swept down from the ceiling and the mermaid fire crackled brightly.

As the feast ended Electra slipped down from the table and went to join Sasha, Nerissa and Sam.

'You look really pretty in that robe,' Nerissa told her as she came over.

Sasha grinned at her. 'Yeah. I'm glad you got to be Queen. I'd have liked to be, but you deserved it, Electra. If it hadn't been for you, those sharks might have eaten us.'

'You were great,' Sam said. 'I don't know how you dared to frighten those sharks.'

'Well, I didn't do it on my own,' Electra said. 'I had Splash, and the giant squid helped.' Guilt flickered across her mind as she thought about the poor squid. It had been so frightened. She glanced at the table where the cake was being given out. 'Hang on! I'll be back in a minute,' she told her friends.

She swam to the table and took the biggest slice of cake. Then she hurried to the cave where the Dana

squid was hiding in its crevasse
again. Electra placed the cake beside
it.

'I'm sorry I frightened you,' she

whispered. 'Thanks for helping us. I hope you like cake.'

She swam quietly away. Outside the cave the musicians had started to play and people were beginning to dance. Reaching the cave entrance, Electra looked back. The squid had opened its eye and was watching her.

It looked at her for a moment and then it winked.

'Bye!' Electra grinned at it. And, swimming out of the cave, she raced to join her friends at the party.

Do you love magic, unicorns and fairies?

Join the sparkling

Linda Chapman

fan club today!

It's FREE!

You will receive a sparkle pack, including:

Stickers   **Badge**
Membership card   **Glittery pencil**

Plus four Linda Chapman newsletters every year,
packed full of fun, games, news and competitions.
And look out for a special card on your birthday!

How to join:

Visit lindachapman.co.uk and enter your details

Send your name, address, date of birth* and email address (if you have one) to:
**Linda Chapman Fan Club, Puffin Marketing,
80 Strand, London, WC2R 0RL**